This book belongs to:

....

First published 2023 by Macmillan Children's Books
an imprint of Pan Macmillan
The Smithson, 6 Briset Street, London EC1M 5NR
EU representative: Macmillan Publishers Ireland Limited,
1st Floor, The Liffey Trust Centre, 117–126 Sheriff Street Upper, Dublin 1, D01 YC43
Associated companies throughout the world.
www.panmacmillan.com

ISBN: 978-1-0350-0527-7

Written by Amanda Li, based on a story by Sam Barlow and Adam Long.
Text and illustrations based on stories and characters created by Colin Williams.
© SIXTEEN SOUTH and Letko 2023
Paper texture page 5 © iStock.com/tomograf

1 3 5 7 9 8 6 4 2

A CIP catalogue record is available for this book from the British Library.

Printed and bound in Great Britain by Bell and Bain Ltd, Glasgow

FSC
www.fsc.org

MIX
Paper | Supporting
responsible forestry
FSC® C116313

ODO
The Egg

Macmillan Children's Books

Say hello to Odo and his friends!

Every day, Odo's parents drop him off at Forest Camp – a forest school for birds where Odo and his friends play, craft and learn!

Doodle

Odo's best friend, a sweet and thoughtful little bird who always wants to help out.

Rosie and Ruby

Two shy flamingos with bright pink feathers. They can be a bit clumsy, but love playing football.

Odo

A little owl with lots of energy who believes anything is possible! He is the only owl at Forest Camp because – unlike most owls – he is awake during the day.

Inspector Feathers

A very old and wise eagle who was the previous Camp Leader. She is now retired – mostly!

Camp Leader

A large eagle who is in charge of Forest Camp. She might seem a bit stern, but she's always very kind.

Pigeon Post

The mail bird, he often drops by with letters and parcels. He loves any excuse for a cup of tea and a chat.

Anna and Rudi

Identical twin swans who do everything together. They are two of the biggest birds in camp and think they are very grown up.

Leonardo
the peacock

Buzz and Zing
the hummingbirds

Flo, Jo and Shirley
the chickens

Thelma
the thrush

Bud and Louie
the toucans

Zu, Bea and Doo
the canaries

John John
the parrot

It was morning, and time for Odo to go to Forest Camp.
"Have a great day, little one!" said his dad.

Odo's friend, Doodle,
was already there.
"Hey, Doodle," said Odo.

"Hi Odo!" said Doodle.

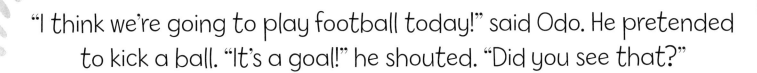

"I think we're going to play football today!" said Odo. He pretended to kick a ball. "It's a goal!" he shouted. "Did you see that?"

"Your invisible ball?" replied Doodle.

Thump! A real football whizzed through the air and hit Odo on the head. Ouch!

"*Now* I can see it!" said Doodle.

"Sorry, Odo!" said a voice. It was Anna, the swan. She was playing football with some of the other birds.

Odo grabbed the football.
"Can I play?" he asked, excitedly. "Please?"

Along came Ruby, the flamingo. "This is a game for **BIG** birds!" she said, snatching the ball back. The big birds ran off, laughing.

Odo and Doodle watched, feeling sad. Why wouldn't the big birds let the little birds play?

Camp Leader flew in and everyone gathered round. "Good morning, campers!" she cried.

"As you know, we birds are all different sizes. Some of us are big, like the swans, and some are little, like Odo. But whatever our size, we all come from EGGS!"

She showed everyone a pile
of smooth, grey eggs.

"These are pretend eggs, made of
rock, but you must look after them
very carefully, just like real eggs."

All the birds took a rock egg.
"Now, off you fly!" said Camp Leader.

Odo soon began to get bored of looking after his egg.
He wanted to do something fun!

"Look, Doodle!" he shouted as he ran past her,
kicking his egg along super-fast.

"Watch out!" cried Doodle.

"It's just a rock!" said Odo, bouncing the egg on the ground.

Then he spotted the flamingos, Ruby and Rosie. "Hey, Rosie," shouted Odo. "I'm going for a **goal!**" He kicked his egg hard.

Whee! Odo's egg flew through the air and landed in the bushes. He didn't notice it roll straight past a REAL egg lying on the ground.

Odo hopped into the bushes
to look for his egg.
"There it is!" he cried.

"I can't wait to see how you're
taking care of your rock eggs,
Campers!" called Camp Leader.

Odo kicked the egg on to the grass. Then he took a big jump and landed – **thud!** – on top of the egg.

Uh-oh! What was happening? Odo looked down. The egg was cracking!

"Oh no!" said Doodle. "How did you crack your rock egg, Odo?"

"I don't know!" said Odo, in a panic.

Along came Camp Leader. She checked Doodle's egg first.
"Excellent egg handling, Doodle!" she said.

Odo was next. He quickly covered up the crack with a large leaf.
"My egg's just having a little sleep," he said.

Just then, Pigeon Post arrived with his sack of mail.

"I'll be back shortly!" said Camp Leader to Odo,
going off to make Pigeon Post a cup of tea.

Craaack!

The egg began to open. Odo and Doodle stared as a head popped out of the top!

All the birds gasped in amazement. "Why is a baby bird inside a rock?" cried one of the chickens.

"**Da da?**" chirped the baby bird, looking at Odo. It hopped out of the egg. It was very big for a baby - even bigger than Odo!

"Nothing to see here," said Odo, trying to calm everyone down. "Just a baby bird that - er - came out of a rock . . ."

"That isn't a rock," said Doodle. "That's a **REAL EGG!**"

The baby bird hopped towards Odo and pecked at him.
"Hey, stop pecking me!" said Odo, giggling.

"It's eating a pine cone!" said Ruby, pointing at the baby bird.

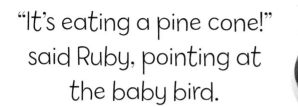

"A pine cone is not for eating," said Odo. "It's for playing. Look!"

Odo threw the pine cone into the air and bounced it on his head. Then he bounced it to the baby bird. Soon they were heading it to each other like footballers!

"Kick the ball to me, Odo!" cried Anna.

"But this is a game for LITTLE birds," said Odo with a smile. Anna looked sad.

"Just kidding!" said Odo, laughing.

He kicked the pine cone to Anna. Soon all the birds, big and little, were joining in the game. It didn't matter what size anyone was – they all had fun together.

Along came Camp Leader.
"Odo, did you take care of your rock egg
and never let it out of your sight?" she asked.

"Yes!" said Odo. "Well . . . I did kick it into
the bushes, but I found it right away."

"Oh, Odo," said Camp Leader. "When you lost your rock egg, I think you accidentally picked up an eagle's egg. It must have fallen from its nest!"

Odo was amazed. "An eagle's egg?" he said. The baby eagle chirped.

Suddenly, a large, important-looking
eagle flew down from the sky.
"Hello, Inspector Feathers!" said Camp Leader.

Inspector Feathers picked up the baby. "Who found this baby eagle?" she asked.

"Er – me," said Odo, nervously.

Inspector Feathers looked at Odo. "This is Eaglet, my little grand-bird," she said. "We thought we'd lost him. Thank you, Odo, for looking after him so well!"

Odo was so happy.
"I knew I could do this!"
he said, giving Eaglet a hug.

"Now Eaglet needs to go
and meet his real mum and
dad," said Camp Leader.

"Can Eaglet come back for a visit one day?" asked Odo.

"Any time!" said Inspector Feathers, with a smile.

Camp Leader's Tips for Grown-ups

In the forest, as in life, the most important thing you can do is to believe in yourself.

Although Odo is one of the littlest campers at Forest Camp, he knows he can do anything he sets his mind to! This book has been specially created for preschool children to help encourage confidence and self-belief.

- Odo and his friends are all different – some are big, some are small; some are loud and some are quiet – but at Forest Camp, they learn to celebrate the things that make them unique.

- As children enter their preschool years, they begin to explore new environments outside of their homes, just like Odo! Reading stories is the perfect way to encounter new situations in a safe and fun way.

- Sharing books and reading together helps children to communicate and to develop ideas and understanding.

- This story is based on an episode of *Odo*. There are lots more episodes you can watch. They have been developed to help build self-confidence and independence.

After you have read this book with your child, you could talk to them about things that happened in the story.
Try talking about . . .

. . . how excited Odo was to go to Forest Camp. Is your child excited to go to nursery or school? What do they like doing best while they are there?

. . . how Odo and Doodle felt when the big birds wouldn't let them play football. What makes your child feel better when they're sad?

. . . what they would do if they had a rock egg to take care of. Why not encourage them to practise taking care of a doll or toy?

. . . how Odo makes a new friend when baby Eaglet hatches from the egg. Talk to your child about their friends. What do they like best about them? What do they enjoy doing together?